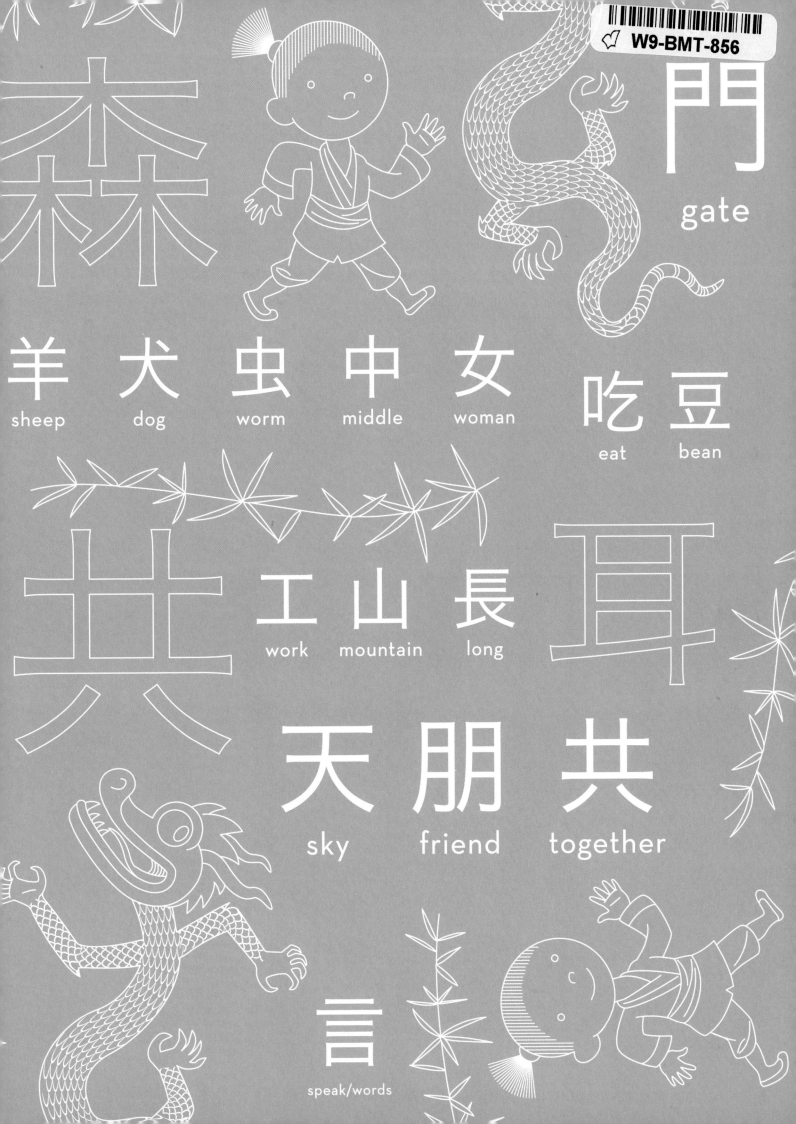

門 gate

羊 sheep

犬 dog

虫 worm

中 middle

女 woman

吃 eat

豆 bean

工 work

山 mountain

長 long

天 sky

朋 friend

共 together

言 speak/words

The Pet Dragon

A Story about Adventure, Friendship, and Chinese Characters

Christoph Niemann

Greenwillow Books
An Imprint of HarperCollinsPublishers

For 腓特烈, 古斯塔夫, and 亞瑟

The Pet Dragon
A Story about Adventure, Friendship, and Chinese Characters
Copyright © 2008 by Christoph Niemann
All rights reserved. Printed in the United States of America.
www.harpercollinschildrens.com

Adobe Illustrator was used to prepare the full-color art.
The text type is Neutra.

Library of Congress Cataloging-in-Publication Data
Niemann, Christoph.
The pet dragon: a story about adventure, friendship,
and Chinese characters /
by Christoph Niemann.
p. cm.
"Greenwillow Books."
Summary: When Lin's beloved pet dragon disappears, she searches for
him far and wide until a witch helps her to reach the dragon's new home.
Introduces a different Chinese character on each step of
Lin's adventure.
ISBN 978-0-06-157776-5 (trade bdg.)—ISBN 978-0-06-157777-2 (lib. bdg.)
[1. Dragons—Fiction. 2. Pets—Fiction. 3. Witches—Fiction. 4. Adventure
and adventurers—Fiction. 5. Chinese characters—Fiction.] I. Title.
PZ7.N56848Pet 2008
[E]—dc22 2007050883

First Edition 10 9 8 7 6 5 4

 Greenwillow Books

Dear Reader,

On a recent trip to Asia, I learned my first Chinese characters. The ones that I could remember most easily were those that are little icons of what they mean (such as 人 = *person*), or the ones that show an idea (you put that person in a box and you will get 囚, which means *prisoner*).

I had a lot of fun imagining connections between characters and their meanings. For instance, 父 means *father*, and even though the character evolved from an image of a man holding a staff or ax and historically refers to a man's social status, all I could see was a grim-looking face with a mustache.

Chinese is a very complex language (one has to know three to four thousand characters to be considered literate). The purpose of this book is not to teach you and your children your first Chinese lesson but rather to give you a glimpse into the fascinating world of the Chinese language and maybe—by making it a little less intimidating—to inspire you and your kids to take a class and learn more.

The Pet Dragon would not have been possible without the inspiration, support, insight, and patience of many people. I want to thank Chika Azuma, Anni Kuan, Lisa Zeitz, Nicholas Blechman, Naomi Mizusaki, Shi Yeon Kim, Liz Darhansoff, and of course Paul Sahre, who taught me 大, the first character I learned. Finally, I am most grateful to Ling-Yi Chien of the Asia Society of New York, whose tremendous knowledge of Chinese language and culture was absolutely essential to the creation of this book.

—Christoph Niemann

This is Lin.

人

person

One day, Lin received a very special gift—
a baby dragon!

小
small

Lin and her pet dragon
did everything together.
They played hide-and-seek.

木
tree

林
woods

森
forest

They made new friends.

牛 羊 犬 虫
cow sheep dog worm

They perfected their Ping-Pong skills.

中
middle

They told each other exciting stories.

女
woman

士
warrior
/gentleman

The dragon loved to play soccer.
"Uh-oh!" cried Lin. She saw the ball
sail toward an old vase.

eye

Crash!

The vase burst into a hundred pieces.

耳

ear

Lin knew that they were in trouble. Big, BIG trouble!

父
father

"From now on your dragon
must stay in a cage!"
said Lin's father.

Lin wasn't very happy
about this . . . and neither
was the baby dragon.

prisoner

The next morning when Lin went to
check on her pet, the cage was empty.
Oh, no! Her dragon was gone!

mouth

Lin couldn't believe it.
"Where is my baby dragon?
Where did my dragon go?"
Lin had to find it!

speak/words

First, Lin searched her house. No dragon.

Then she searched her entire city. No dragon.

Where could her dragon be?

She started walking . . .

工
work

門
gate

and walking and walking.

mountain

Lin came to a huge wall that stretched
all the way to the horizon.
She looked and she looked and she looked.

長

But still there was
no sign of her dragon.

長
long

Lin came to a wide river. She saw a curious little lady standing near the edge of the water.

"My dear girl," the lady said, in a cackling voice.

"I need to get to the other side, but I can't swim. Help! Please lift me up!"

巫
witch/shaman

川

river

So Lin did, and she carried
the little lady across the river.

上 下
above　below

Lin set the witch down gently on the other side.

"Dear little one," the witch said, "a favor deserves a favor.

I know where to find what you are looking for."

Zaapp! A jar appeared in the witch's hand.

豆

水

水
water

豆
bean

She removed a magic bean from the jar
and popped it in her mouth.
She chewed it very slowly.
She began to shake and rumble!

吃
eat

The little witch started to grow and grow and grow.
Soon she was as tall as a mountain!
"Come here, little Lin," she said, her voice booming.
"I am going to help you find your friend."

大
big

And she lifted Lin
through the clouds!

天
sky

Lin couldn't believe her eyes.
There was her dragon,
all grown up and beautiful.
Was this the dragon's true home
and the dragon's real family?

朋
friend

Whoosh! The dragon flew Lin all the way
back to the city where she lived.
The two friends made plans to visit often.

Lin's father was so happy to see his daughter!
He thanked the dragon for bringing Lin home and
promised the two friends that they could play together
whenever they wanted. Then they celebrated!

共
together

人 person

小 small

口 mouth

上 above

下 below

士 warrior/gentleman

目 eye

囚 prisoner

父 father

水 water

牛 cow

父

木 tree

林 woods

森 forest

小

大 big

耳 ear

巫 witch/shaman

川 river